I Thought I Could and I Did

BOBBIE PARROTT

Copyright © 2015 Bobbie Parrott.

All rights reserved. No part of this book may be used or reproduced by any means, graphic, electronic, or mechanical, including photocopying, recording, taping or by any information storage retrieval system without the written permission of the author except in the case of brief quotations embodied in critical articles and reviews.

Balboa Press books may be ordered through booksellers or by contacting:

Balboa Press
A Division of Hay House
1663 Liberty Drive
Bloomington, IN 47403
www.balboapress.com
1 (877) 407-4847

Because of the dynamic nature of the Internet, any web addresses or links contained in this book may have changed since publication and may no longer be valid. The views expressed in this work are solely those of the author and do not necessarily reflect the views of the publisher, and the publisher hereby disclaims any responsibility for them.

Any people depicted in stock imagery provided by Thinkstock are models,
and such images are being used for illustrative purposes only.
Certain stock imagery © Thinkstock.

ISBN: 978-1-5043-4129-5 (sc)
ISBN: 978-1-5043-4130-1 (e)

Library of Congress Control Number: 2015915661

Print information available on the last page.

Balboa Press rev. date: 10/1/2015

I Thought I Could and I Did

BOBBIE PARROTT

When I was a baby, I thought I could learn to feed myself.

And I did!

I thought I could walk by myself.

And I did !

When I was a little older, I thought I could go to school by myself.

And I did!

Then I thought I could learn to ride a bike.

And I did!

THEN I thought I could play hockey.

And I did!

When I was 12, I thought I could bake cookies by myself.

And I did!

Now I am older, and I thought I could write a book for kids to read.

And I did !

Now it's your turn.

"Put your picture here."

What do you think you can do?

Let's have some fun. Email me at ithoughticould2015@gmail.com and tell me what you did. I'd love to hear from you!

Bobbie

CPSIA information can be obtained
at www.ICGtesting.com
Printed in the USA
LVOW05s1911301015
460511LV00010B/21/P

9 781504 341295